MOLLY'S Great Discovery

A Book About Dyslexia and Self-Advocacy

by Krista Weltner

free spirit
PUBLISHING®

Special thanks to the entire team at Free Spirit Publishing, my Fabulous Critique Group, Christopher Miller, Fernette and Brock Eide, and the Oregon and Dallas branches of the International Dyslexia Association for all your support and help in making my dream a reality.

Text and illustrations copyright © 2024 by Krista Weltner

All rights reserved under international and Pan-American Copyright Conventions. Unless otherwise noted, no part of this book may be reproduced, stored in a retrieval system, or transmitted in any form or by any means, electronic, mechanical, photocopying, recording or otherwise, without express written permission from the publisher, except for brief quotations and critical reviews. For more information, go to freespirit.com/permissions.

Free Spirit, Free Spirit Publishing, and associated logos are trademarks and/or registered trademarks of Teacher Created Materials. A complete listing of our logos and trademarks is available at freespirit.com.

Library of Congress Cataloging-in-Publication Data
Names: Weltner, Krista, author, illustrator.
Title: Molly's great discovery : a book about dyslexia and self-advocacy / by Krista Weltner.
Description: Huntington Beach : Free Spirit Publishing, 2024. | Series: Everyday adventures with Molly and dyslexia ; book 1 | Audience: Ages 4¬–8.
Identifiers: LCCN 2023016848 (print) | LCCN 2023016849 (ebook) | ISBN 9798885540254 (hardback) | ISBN 9798885540261 (ebook) | ISBN 9798885540278 (epub)
Subjects: CYAC: Dyslexia—Fiction. | Friendship—Fiction. | Schools—Fiction. | BISAC: JUVENILE FICTION / Neurodiversity | JUVENILE FICTION / Social Themes / Emotions & Feelings | LCGFT: Picture books.
Classification: LCC PZ7.1.W43563 Mu 2024 (print) | LCC PZ7.1.W43563 (ebook) | DDC [E]—dc23
LC record available at https://lccn.loc.gov/2023016848
LC ebook record available at https://lccn.loc.gov/2023016849

Free Spirit Publishing does not have control over or assume responsibility for author or third-party websites and their content. Parents, teachers, and other adults: We strongly urge you to monitor children's use of the internet.

Edited by Cassie Sitzman
Cover and interior design by Colleen Pidel

Printed in China

Free Spirit Publishing
An imprint of Teacher Created Materials
9850 51st Avenue North, Suite 100
Minneapolis, MN 55442
(612) 338-2068
help4kids@freespirit.com
freespirit.com

FSC
www.fsc.org
MIX
Paper | Supporting responsible forestry
FSC® C144853

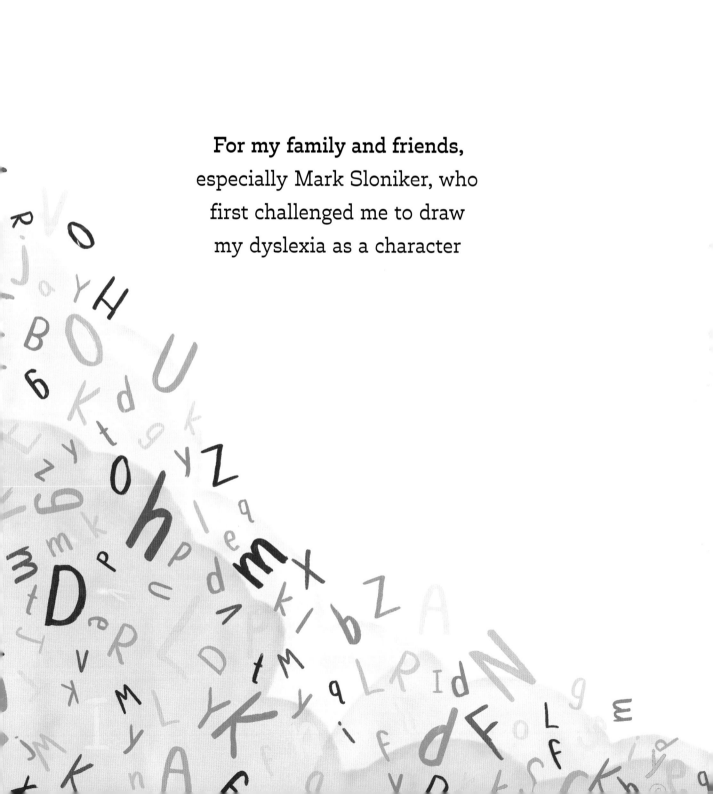

For my family and friends,
especially Mark Sloniker, who
first challenged me to draw
my dyslexia as a character

There is an invisible part of Molly that nobody else knows about. Molly calls her Lexi.

Molly and Lexi have
a big imagination.

They like to play
games, solve problems,
and learn new things.

But learning to read is challenging for Molly and Lexi. Learning to spell is even harder. They practice as much as they can for the spelling test.

They only get a few words right. Just like last week, and the week before that.

Mr. Mitchell is always encouraging. "Keep at it, Molly. You're a smart kid."

"Ask Mr. Mitchell for help," suggests Lexi.

"I don't know what to say. The words won't come out right," Molly sighs.

When Molly writes, she has so many ideas and important thoughts. But she can't seem to put them on paper.

"Pleeeeeease ask Mr. Mitchell for help!" begs Lexi.

"If I do that, everyone will think I'm dumb," Molly moans.

During quiet reading time, Molly sees how fast the other kids fly through their books. "It's like they have a superpower that I don't."

"Ask for help!" says Lexi.

But Molly just turns the pages quickly and pretends to read. "I don't want anyone to know I'm different," she explains.

Mr. Mitchell interrupts quiet reading with an announcement. "Today, we're going to practice reading out loud."

"I can't do this,"
Molly whispers.

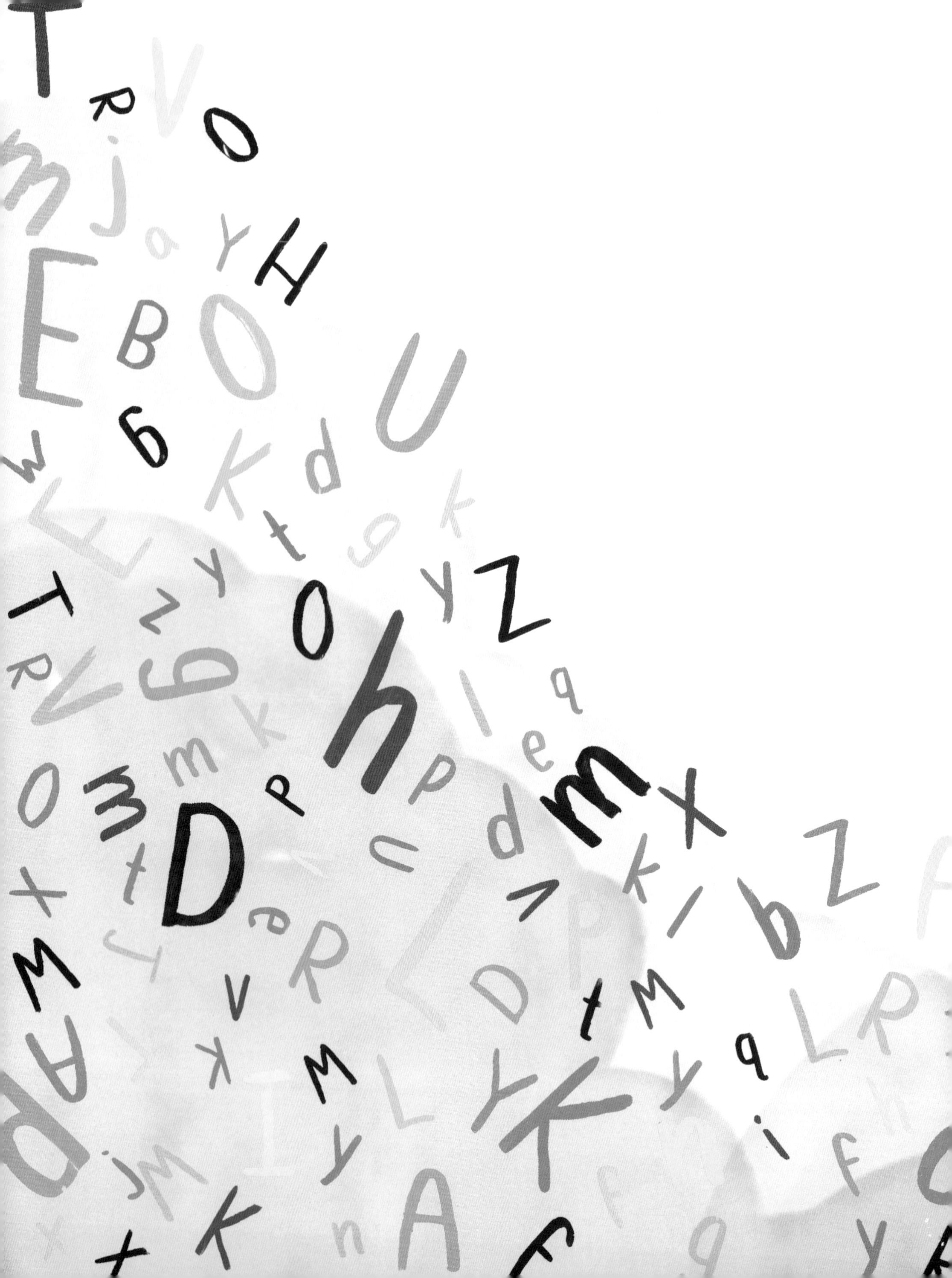

"I wish I could run from it.
I wish I could hide from it."

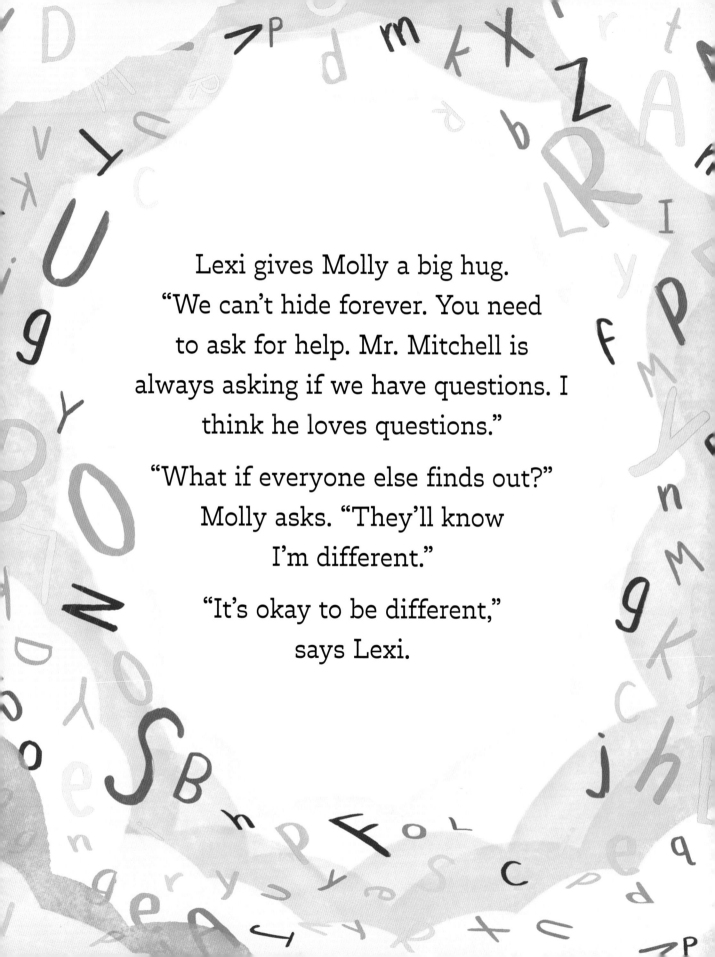

Lexi gives Molly a big hug.
"We can't hide forever. You need
to ask for help. Mr. Mitchell is
always asking if we have questions. I
think he loves questions."

"What if everyone else finds out?"
Molly asks. "They'll know
I'm different."

"It's okay to be different,"
says Lexi.

With a big breath, Molly and Lexi march up
to Mr. Mitchell.

"Can you help me with my reading and spelling?" Molly asks.

"I'm so glad you asked for help," says Mr. Mitchell. "That is very brave."

Mr. Mitchell introduces Molly to a teacher named Ms. Feltz.

For one afternoon, Molly gets to play games, take reading tests, and do fun puzzles.

After that, Ms. Feltz knows why Molly has trouble in reading and spelling.

Molly has dyslexia.

Ms. Feltz explains that dyslexia is a learning
disability. It makes spelling, reading, and writing
extra challenging. It also makes Molly extra
creative and smart in ways kids without dyslexia
might not be. Ms. Feltz tells Molly that lots of
people are dyslexic.

Everyone has a unique way of thinking and doing things.

Some differences are on the outside, and some are on the inside.

Molly and Lexi finally understand.

Now Molly gets the help she needs in the learning center.

Lots of other kids do too. Some need extra help with math, handwriting, speaking, or reading. And some need a quiet space to take a test or do their work.

Each has their own invisible difference.

Back in Mr. Mitchell's classroom, Molly and Lexi feel much better. They get more spelling words right. They read at their own pace.

And when Molly needs a little extra help, she asks for it.

A Note to Readers

A friend once challenged me to draw my dyslexia as a character for an illustration contest. I drew an image of a girl, squished into a desk, happily working with her dyslexia—a purple cloud of alphabet letters with a face and big glasses. I began to imagine my dyslexia with a personality and spirit. What would I say to her? This became the inspiration for the characters Molly and Lexi. I wanted to create a series that could help you explore how you feel about your own differences, especially if you are dyslexic.

Today, I would tell my dyslexia how much I love and appreciate her. I would thank her for making me strong, creative, and intelligent, and for being such a big part of my life. But I didn't always appreciate being dyslexic.

Seven-year-old me would have had a much different conversation with her learning difference. I would have told my dyslexia how frustrated she made me. I might have even told her to go away and leave me alone and that I wished she didn't exist. But dyslexia isn't a temporary condition or something that can be wished away. Dyslexia is a huge part of who I am. I now know how important it has been in my success as an author and artist, and how much better life is when you love all the parts of yourself. I wish I had felt kinder toward my learning difference as a kid. I hope you enjoy this series and learn to love all your wonderful differences, whether you're dyslexic or not. I hope you learn to appreciate the many ways you and your friends and classmates learn and see the world. I hope you celebrate your triumphs and your challenges. And I hope you know how brilliant you are and how your differences are part of what makes you wonderfully you.

—Krista

A Word About Terms

You may have heard dyslexia referred to in a variety of ways. In this series, I use terms like *dyslexic*, *dyslexia*, *learning difference*, *invisible difference*, and *learning disability*. All people have a right to choose how they want to talk about their differences and the words they are comfortable with. The terms in this series may not work for everyone, and people's preferences can vary based on where they live and the communities they are part of. I chose to describe Molly as "being dyslexic" as well as "having dyslexia." For me, it is essential to include identity-first language because it emphasizes how Molly's dyslexia is a core part of her. These terms reflect how I speak about my own dyslexia as well.

Learn More About Dyslexia
The International Dyslexia Association (dyslexiaida.org)
Dyslexic Advantage (dyslexicadvantage.org)
The Yale Center for Dyslexia and Creativity (dyslexia.yale.edu)

A Note for Adults: Helping Children Self-Advocate

I was diagnosed with dyslexia when I was seven after my second-grade teacher noticed I wasn't making the progress he expected in reading and spelling. I feel incredibly grateful and privileged to have been given the early intervention and support that I so desperately needed and that so many children never receive.

Even with the support of my teachers, I, like Molly, still had to learn early how to ask for help and tell adults what I needed—I had to self-advocate, and often! Self-advocacy is a useful skill for all children, but especially for those with learning differences. I hope this book promotes conversation around reaching out for help when we need it and what dyslexia is all about.

Here are a few tips for helping all children learn to self-advocate.

Talk About Learning and Thinking Differences

It may be difficult at first, but it's important to talk with children about learning differences they or people they know have. If kids have a diagnosis, they may or may not know the clinical term. That's okay. What's most important is that children know there is nothing wrong with talking about what they struggle to learn and how that affects them. It's easier for kids to self-advocate and ask for help when they know it is safe to talk about the different ways they think and learn.

Identify Children's Strengths

In addition to talking about struggles, help children identify their strengths. Everyone has things that feel more natural or easy for them. Identifying strengths gives children the confidence to talk about what they're good at. Guide children to remember these strengths when they feel stuck in their struggles.

Some of the researched-backed dyslexic strengths highlighted in the Everyday Adventures with Molly & Dyslexia series include creativity, problem-solving, material reasoning, empathy, big-picture thinking, narrative reasoning, and three-dimensional thinking.

Encourage Children's Questions

Children might feel nervous about asking too many questions, especially if they haven't yet grown confidence in talking about how they think and learn or if they think their questions might draw attention to a learning difference. Create a culture in your home or classroom where children's questions are welcomed—and celebrated! Ask questions yourself about things you don't know or have wondered about, and invite children to help you find answers.

Get excited about children's questions and investigate them together. Be proactive in offering help when you notice children struggling, and encourage them to speak up when they don't understand. Let kids know that they can come to you privately if they don't feel comfortable asking in front of the group.

Role-Play Asking for Help

Children may not feel comfortable asking adults for help or accommodations. Remind children that adults are there to help them, and talk about when and how to ask. Role-play scenarios where a child might need or want to ask for help, and provide ideas for how they can start a request. Practicing what to say when asking for help can be a wonderful way to help children grow confidence in this skill.

About the Author and Illustrator

Krista Weltner is an author, illustrator, filmmaker, and puppet fabricator. The Everyday Adventures with Molly & Dyslexia series marks her publishing debut. In addition to her literary pursuits, she works in the stop-motion film industry. Her work can be seen in Netflix Animation's *Wendell and Wild* and in LAIKA Studios's *Wildwood*. Her short film, *Partially Compensated*, which is also inspired by her experiences growing up with dyslexia, has been shown at film festivals around the world and has afforded her numerous opportunities to engage and advocate with others for a more inclusive world.